P9-ECL-801

We All Sing with the Same Voice

We All Sing with

the Same Voice

By J. Philip Miller and Sheppard M. Greene
Illustrated by Paul Meisel

HARPERCOLLINS*PUBLISHERS*

My hair is black and red.

My hair is yellow.

My eyes are brown and green and blue.

My name is Jack and Fred.

My name's Amanda Sue.
I'm called Kareem Abdu.
My name is *you*.

I live in southern France.

I'm from a Texas ranch.

I come from Mecca and Peru.

I live across the street,

In the mountains,

On the beach.

I come from everywhere,

And my name is you.

We all sing with the same voice,
The same song,
The same voice.

We all sing with the same voice,
And we sing in harmony.

Sometimes I get mad and mean.

Sometimes I feel happy.

And when I want to cry I do.

When I'm by myself at night,
I hold my teddy tight,
Until the morning light.
My name is you.

I have sisters one two three.
In my family there's just me.

I've got one daddy.
I've got two.

Grandpa helps me cross the street.

My cat walks on furry feet.

I love my parakeet.
My name is you.

We all sing with the same voice,
The same song,
The same voice.
We all sing with the same voice,
And we sing in harmony.

I like to run and climb.

I like to sit and read.

I like to watch my TV too.

And when it's time for bed,

I like my stories read,

"Sweet dreams" and "love you" said.

My name is you.

We all sing with the same voice,
The same song,
The same voice.

We all sing with the same voice,
And we sing in harmony.

For Ram
—P.M.

 For information address HarperCollins Children's Books, a division of HarperCollins Publishers, 1350 Avenue of the Americas, New York, NY 10019. www.harperchildrens.com

Typography by Hui Hui Su-Kennedy
1 2 3 4 5 6 7 8 9 10
❖
First Edition